Disney Girls

Good-bye, Jasmine?

Gabrielle Charbonnet

Disney
PRESS

NEW YORK

Printed in the United States of America.

First Edition

1   3   5   7   9   10   8   6   4   2

The text of this book is set in 15-point Adobe Garamond.

Library of Congress Catalog Card Number: 98-88405

ISBN: 0-7868-4273-3

For more Disney Press fun, visit www.DisneyBooks.com

Contents

Disney Girls

Good-bye, Jasmine?

Chapter One

Summertime's Cool!

"Look at this one," Isabelle Beaumont said, holding up a ceramic bead. She leaned against the side of my bed.

"Cool," I told her. I scooted over and pawed through the storage tray. I needed a bead with yellow in it.

"Mine is finished. I'm going to tie it around my ankle," said Ariel Ramos.

My five best friends and I were in my room, we had a whole new box of cool beads, we were together. . . . Everything in my life seemed fabulous, right at that instant. It was like pure magic. Have you ever had that feeling?

"I'm glad to be back," I told my friends.

"We're glad to have you back," said Ella O'Connor, stringing a lavender bead.

"Yeah," said Yukiko Hayashi. "It was a long month without you. And your pool."

I grinned. Isabelle, Paula Pinto, Ella, Yukiko, and Ariel all live in a suburb of Orlando, Florida, called Willow Hill. I live in a house in Wildwood Estates, and we have our own pool. It's covered, so my friends I can swim all year long. Especially during Orlando's endless, hot summers, we go swimming almost every day.

My friends hadn't been to my pool the whole month of June, because my parents and I had been in Europe since the day after our school had let out. (The six of us go to Orlando Elementary.) For a whole month, Mother and Daddy and I had been traveling around Italy, France, and England. It had been great, but now I was glad to be home again. I love traveling, but I also love coming home.

One of the best things about coming home was getting caught up with my friends. They'd been doing cool things all June, and I had missed everything. Paula had been helping at her mom's veterinary office. Ariel had been practicing some tricky new dives during swim team practice, three days a week. Ella had been fixing up her room, with her stepmother's help.

"Which country was your favorite?" asked Paula. She tried on her beaded headband over her dark hair.

"Um, I loved the food in Italy and France," I said. "England was gorgeous—beautiful and green. There are really old houses everywhere. And castles," I continued. "I loved the castles. And France was so great because Belle was with me."

Isabelle and I smiled at each other. She had actually joined my parents and me in France for a whole week! We'd had an incredible, magical time.

"But Italy was awesome too," I mused. "We were in the south, where it's hot and dry. I felt really at home there."

My five friends nodded.

"France was so amazing," Isabelle said. Now she was attaching tiny gold beads to the ends of each of her little braids. She's African American, and wears her hair in all sorts of incredible, interesting ways. Today she had a hundred little braids. With gold beads on them, she'd look like a princess. (Actually, she *is* a princess. But I'll explain about that later.)

I have long, boring, straight blond hair.

"We know," said Ariel. "You've told us about it like a thousand times."

I laughed, and Isabelle tossed a pillow at Ariel.

"Careful, careful!" Ella cried. "Don't knock over the beads!"

I clasped my arms around my knees. I had missed my friends so much while I was gone! But we would have two whole months together, and then we'd be at school together in the fall.

"Oh, hey, Paula," I said. "You have to show me everything you learned at the dojo while I was gone." I turned to Yukiko. "And you have to get me all caught up about what's happening at Madame Pavlova's."

Paula and I take tae kwan do at a dojo in Willow Hill. Tae kwan do is a type of karate. A dojo is a place where you study it. I looove tae kwan do. Before I had gone on vacation, I'd already earned my yellow belt.

And Yukiko and I take ballet together at Madame Pavlova's. During the school year, we go only once a week. In the summertime, we go twice a week. And I take karate twice a week too. My summer was getting booked up fast!

"We learned an awesome new kata last week," said Paula, springing to her feet. "Let me show you." (A kata is kind of like a choreographed dance, except with karate moves. We have to learn a lot of them.)

Just as Paula began to concentrate and move slowly through the motions, my bedroom door pushed open, and my kitten, Rajah, padded in. He gave Paula a look like, why are you even trying to be graceful? You're not a cat.

He caught Paula's eye, and she stopped dead. "Oh my stars," she exclaimed. "Is that Rajah?"

I stared at her as I scratched behind Rajah's orange ears.

"Of course it's Rajah," I said. "Who else would it be? I have only one kitten."

"Jasmine," said Isabelle, "that is not a kitten. That is like, a mountain lion."

I looked down at my pet. He was the same familiar Rajah he had always been. "What?" I asked, as Rajah flopped over so I could rub his tummy.

"What did Mrs. Perth feed him while you were gone?" Yukiko asked, giggling. "He's enormous!" (Mrs. Perth is my family's housekeeper. She's terrific.)

I cocked my head. Well, maybe he *had* grown a little. "He's just my little bitty baby," I crooned to him while he purred.

Ella tried to smother a laugh, and ending up snorting like a rhino with a cold. "Your bitty baby must weigh as much as I do," she choked out.

"He's a *whale*," Ariel said bluntly. "If you took him to the beach, people would try to rescue him and drag him back into the ocean."

My five best friends were snickering and chuckling at my poor little weensy baby kitten, and all I could do was glare at them.

It felt great to be home.

Chapter Two

A Family Tradition

"Pack it up," I sang under my breath. I grabbed my nightgown and shoved it into my duffel. I had the Honeygirls cranked on my CD player, and I was dancing and singing along to "Just Let It Out."

I twirled over to my dresser and pulled out a pair of shorts. "Pack it up," I sang. "You've got to pack it up, pack up those bad feelings, then let it out, let out those good vibes . . ." I paused for a moment to do a little dance move in front of my mirror. I looked fabulous.

It was Wednesday, and I was getting ready to go to

Ariel's house for a mid-week Disney Girl* sleepover. Yay, summer! During the school year we can have sleepovers only on the weekends.

"Let out those good vibes," I wailed, shimmying across my room. On the windowseat, Rajah opened one eye to look at me, then closed it again. It takes a lot to disturb his nap.

This was going to be an extra-special DG sleepover, for a bunch of reasons: 1) It was the first sleepover since I'd been back. 2) It was in the middle of the week, which made it feel more fun. 3) Ariel had just gotten the *Mulan* video to watch. 4) For once, Ariel's older sisters, Laurel and Camille, wouldn't be at Ariel's house to bug us. They were both at sleepaway camp. It was a family tradition for kids in the Ramos family to go to Camp Minnechuba in the Appalachian Mountains, every summer. Next summer, when Ariel was nine, she would go too, for four whole weeks! In the meantime, our sleepover was big-sisterless, which was great!

"Say yes to your power," I sang, looking for my hairbrush. A tap on my door interrupted me, and I looked up to see Mother motioning for me to turn the music down.

(*My five friends and I are all Disney Girls—in fact, Disney princesses. I'll explain it as soon as I have time.)

I did.

"Goodness," said Mother. "I bet your poor little eardrums are crying for mercy."

"Is that what Grandmother used to say to you when you were listening to like, the Bee Gees?" I teased her.

Mother giggled. "Yes, I think she did say something like that. And I'm sure you'll say the same thing to your daughter when she's listening to the Horrid Unkempt Thugs, or whoever's popular then."

We laughed together. It was fun thinking about all of us saying the same thing, generation after generation.

Mother sat down on my bed.

"Can you give me a ride over to Ariel's in about twenty minutes?" I asked.

"I'm sorry, honey," said Mother. "My car's making a funny sound. Daddy will take you. But listen, I wanted to talk to you about something first."

I looked up.

"It's about your cat," said Mother. "He's . . . well, he's not a kitten anymore."

I glanced over at Rajah. Okay, okay, he had grown a little. But that's what kittens do. They grow.

"Uh huh," I said.

"So things that used to be acceptable, or even cute, when he was little, are not so cute anymore," Mother continued.

"Like what?" I asked. He still seemed sooo cute to me.

Mother looked unhappy. "Like shredding my brand-new, expensive, beautiful, fiber-art sculpture that was hanging in the foyer," she said. "He sharpened his claws on it, and it's *ruined*. It was a beautiful piece, Jasmine, and I paid a fortune for it because it benefited the Orlando Women's Education Program. Now it just looks like a clump of tangled yarn."

"I'm sorry he did that, Mother," I said. "But actually, it looked like tangled yarn before Rajah got to it."

"It isn't funny, Jazzy," Mother said. "You know how I feel about having animals in the house in the first place. I'd rather we just *visit* animals somewhere else. As long as Rajah is well behaved, he's welcome. But you have to stop him from shredding things. Just yesterday your father noticed the back of his library chair and almost had a conniption."

"I'm sorry," I said again. "I know he shouldn't do stuff like that. Paula knows a lot about animals. I'll ask her for advice."

"Talk to her soon," Mother advised. She stood up. "And maybe you'll develop a greater sense of art appreciation next year, when you go to St. John's."

For several long moments, my brain couldn't process what Mother had said. St. John's Academy was where she had gone to school as a girl. It was a *boarding* school. So what did she—

"Whaaat?" I said.

Mother stood up and folded a T-shirt neatly on my bed. "You know, St. John's," she said casually. "You're nine now, and old enough to attend a boarding school. Goodness, I started there when I was only eight."

"Uh, uh," I stammered stupidly.

Mother finally realized something was wrong, and she looked up at me in surprise. "Why, Jazzy," she said, "you know we've always talked about your attending St. John's. I went there when I was a girl, my mother went there, her mother went there—girls in our family have gone to St. John's Academy since it first opened its doors, back in—"

"Eighteen ninety-two," I said. I had heard the stories hundreds of times. At St. John's, one of the dorms is even called Bingham Hall, after my great-grandmother on my

11

mother's side. (My mom is the former Mary Sue Bingham of the Charlottesville Binghams.)

"But I thought it was just talk, my going there," I continued. I plopped next to Rajah on the windowseat. I realized he took up almost the whole seat by himself. That's a big cat, I thought.

"No, of course not, darling," said Mother. "St. John's is a family tradition. When you were first born, one of the first things I thought was, thank heavens she's a girl, so she can go to St. John's."

"Away? To a boarding school?"

"Oh yes. You'll have a wonderful, marvelous time," Mother assured me. "I had some of the best years of my life at St. John's. You'll treasure the experience, I'm sure. Now let me go ask Daddy if he can run you over to Ariel's." Mother kissed the top of my head and left my room. I sat there next to Rajah's sleeping body, thinking, Oh no, oh no, oh no, oh no. . . .

Chapter Three

I Crush a Sleepover

I was so upset by the time I got to Ariel's house that I couldn't pretend everything was fine. Isabelle took one look at my face and demanded, "What? What happened?"

I sat on Ariel's bed miserably until all the Disney Girls were there. (I know I still have to explain about that. But this is more important. Just hang in there.)

When we were all together, I took a deep breath. If I looked at anyone's eyes, I would just burst into tears, so I looked around Ariel's room instead. The walls are painted in flowing stripes of different shades of blue and green.

Even her window has small panes of blue and green stained glass in it. When the sun shines through them, you feel like you're in an aquarium.

"Just tell us, Jasmine, please," Isabelle said quietly.

"Mother and Daddy are sending me to St. John's Academy in September," I blurted.

Silence.

"The boarding school your mom went to?" Paula clarified.

"Yes," I answered. "Mother started there when she was only eight. So they think I'm old enough."

"Boarding school?" Isabelle repeated, looking shocked. "You mean, you would *live* there?"

"That's what boarding school is," I said grumpily. "St. John's is in South Carolina. Which is a real far way away from Orlando."

Finally I glanced up. Ella, Yukiko, and Paula looked worried and unhappy. Even Ariel couldn't think of a snappy response. But when I met Isabelle's big brown eyes, looking shocked and horrified, that was what did me in. I burst into tears.

Guess what? Having a sleepover where six best friends are

all sobbing and weeping and freaking out is not, as my grandmother would say, a delightful time. When Mrs. Ramos came to tell us the pizza-making stuff was set up, she stopped in the doorway, staring at us in amazement.

"Jasmine's going away to boarding school!" Ariel cried. Hearing her say it out loud made me cry harder.

"Ohhh," said Mrs. Ramos. "When?"

"September," I choked out.

"That's right—your mom went to boarding school herself, didn't she?" asked Mrs. Ramos.

I nodded and blew my nose. "All the girls in my family do. I actually have a cousin who's already there. In eighth grade."

Mrs. Ramos came in and sat next to me on Ariel's bed. I like Mrs. Ramos. She looks a lot like Ariel, with bright red hair and big blue eyes. She's older than my mom, and she doesn't care so much about clothes and fashion and always doing things the way they're supposed to be done. I love my mother just the way she is, but Mrs. Ramos is very comfortable, know what I mean?

Anyway, Mrs. Ramos sat on one side of me and put her arm around me, and Isabelle sat on the other side, crying against my shoulder and making a wet patch on my

T-shirt. (I didn't mind.) Ariel sat next to her mom, and Paula sat next to her. Ella and Yukiko were huddled next to Isabelle on the other side. We were like a miserable, weeping conga line.

After a few moments, Mrs. Ramos said, "You know, crying isn't going to help anything. I think you guys should wash your faces, come downstairs, pig out on pizza, and then, when you're calmer and not hungry, you can think this thing through better. Okay?"

Paula sniffled. "That makes sense."

I nodded. "Sounds good to me."

Mrs. Ramos patted my shoulder and stood up. "Come on, then," she said. "Chuck wagon."

I've noticed that I do think better when my stomach isn't empty. And making our own pizzas took our minds off my impending doom, at least a little bit. Isabelle and I made spinach, garlic, and mushroom pizzas. (We both like interesting foods. None of the others do.) Ariel put extra pepperoni on hers. Yukiko and Ella both put on extra cheese and lots of tomato sauce. Paula made a vegetarian one with extra green peppers.

Afterward, my friends and I felt more ready to tackle

the problem head-on, instead of sitting around crying like a bunch of weenies. (There's nothing wrong with crying. It always makes me feel better. But it's also a good thing to take action on your problems, instead of just worrying about them.)

Back in Ariel's room, with the door closed so her little sister Sophie (she's six) couldn't spy on us, we decided to get serious. Ella took out a notepad and a pen. (She's super-organized. It comes in handy.)

"Okay, suggestions?" Ella asked briskly, writing down a heading on her paper. She showed it to us. It said, "How To Save Jasmine."

"Let's use our magic," said Isabelle immediately. Ella wrote it down. (I *know* I haven't explained yet about the Disney Girls. I *promise* you I will.)

"We need a plan," said Paula, snapping her fingers. "We need to examine all the aspects of the problem."

"How about we, like, pretend Jasmine has been kidnapped," Ariel suggested. "We'll hide her in my closet or something. The ransom will be that her parents have to promise not to send her to boarding school."

We all looked at her.

"Just write it down," Ariel said impatiently.

"How about we blow up St. John's?" Isabelle said sarcastically. "Write *that* down."

"I was just suggesting—" Ariel began.

Paula held up her hands. "Look, guys, we're all working together, okay? Let's just toss out ideas. Later we'll decide which ones are best."

By the time Mrs. Ramos told us to get ready for bed, we had a whole page of ideas. So far the only good one was for us to call on magic. We planned to do that as soon as we turned out the lights. None of the other ideas seemed as if they would do anything besides upset my parents or land us in jail.

The six of us brushed our teeth, put on our nightgowns, and got ready for bed. We were very quiet. It was just about the worst DG sleepover I had ever been to. And it was all my fault.

Chapter Four

Friends = Family

Usually at a Disney Girl sleepover, there is a lot of laughing, playing, singing, dancing, pretending, snacking, dressing up, reading out loud, watching movies, acting out stuff, talking, writing stuff, and so on. Tonight we had watched *Mulan*, talked quietly, made a magic wish, then gone to bed. It might as well have been a school night.

At Ariel's house we usually sleep in the playroom. The playroom is on the third floor—it used to be the attic, but it's all fixed up.

The six of us had spread our sleeping bags on the floor in a big circle. For a while we had talked in the dark, but one by one I heard my friends drift into sleep. Although I felt kind of alone, lying there awake, I didn't feel lonely. Just listening to my friends breathing made me feel better. (I know that sounds weird, but it's true.)

It made me remember how happy I had been to meet them, and how much they mean to me—especially Isabelle. (I'm finally about to explain everything. Are you paying attention?)

From kindergarten to second grade, I went to Greenbriar Academy, which is right here in Wildwood Estates. It's a private school, and it's really gorgeous and expensive and has the best of everything. I liked it okay. The teachers were nice. And the kids were okay, too. But I never felt as if I fit in there—which is weird, because I *should* have fit in there perfectly. I mean, it was a school for rich kids, and I'm a rich kid. Our parents all had the same kinds of jobs. We lived in the same kinds of houses. We rode to school in the same kinds of cars. But I still thought I stuck out like a Honeygirls CD in the Mozart rack, you know? I was just . . . different.

In second grade, my mom signed me up for ballet

classes at Madame Pavlova's Academy of Dance. Mother thought that ballet classes would help me develop grace and poise. To my surprise, I totally got into it. At Madame Pavlova's, I met Yukiko Hayashi. We started chatting before and after classes, and I realized I liked her more than any of my friends from school.

Yukiko was a year younger than me, and went to Orlando Elementary. She told me about her best friend, Ella, and her other friends, Ariel and Paula. They sounded so cool, and seemed to do such neat stuff together. Soon Yukiko and I were hanging out. I was so psyched to be friends with her, but at the same time, there was a wall between us. It felt as if Yukiko was holding back somehow, and not being totally herself. And I had a humongous secret that I couldn't, wouldn't, share with her.

Then one day it happened. We were at her house, and it was totally wild and loud, as usual. Yukiko's six little brothers were marching around, making noise, singing, swinging swords at each other. It reminded me of something.

Just then, Yukiko smiled. "I call them the six Dwarfs," she said. "Because they're all smaller and younger than me. And I guess that makes me Snow White."

I shivered. It was as if a window opened, and I could suddenly see clearly. I remember thinking, *oh my gosh*, kind of breathlessly. Slowly I blinked and looked at Yukiko. And I saw Snow White. Yep. The real Snow White. When I blinked again, Yukiko was back. My mouth dropped open.

I guess Yukiko decided right then to take a chance on me. She told me everything: about how she had always felt different, as if a thread of magic ran through her life. Then she had seen the movie *Snow White*, and it had seemed like a home movie. It was her walking across the screen, running through the woods, making friends with the animals and the Dwarfs. Yukiko felt as if she'd had amnesia, and was just then remembering who she truly was.

I had to agree with her. It made perfect sense to me. After all, her name, Yukiko, means "Snow Child" in Japanese. She has six little brothers, and her mom had another baby last October, making *seven*, for the seven Dwarfs. Most important, Yukiko *felt* like Snow White. She just *was* Snow White.

After she finished, she looked at me, waiting. Seeing if I would laugh nervously or say I had to leave or something. Instead, I said, "Have you ever seen the movie *Aladdin*?"

"Only about a thousand times," said Yukiko.

I spread my arms out. "I'm Jasmine," I said simply. "Princess Jasmine."

Okay, I know what you're thinking: I have blond hair, green eyes, and freckles. I don't exactly look like Princess Jasmine. That doesn't matter. If you really, really, gaze deeply into my eyes, you'll see reflections of round towers, mountains of sand, exotic carpets and jewels and velvet curtains billowing in the hot desert wind.

I took a chance on Yukiko, the way she had taken a chance on me. She looked deeply into my eyes, while I sat still, holding my breath. And she smiled. "Yes," she said. "I see it."

With those four words, my entire life changed forever. Instead of feeling as if I didn't fit in anywhere, didn't belong—well, all of a sudden I was totally accepted. Yukiko truly understood. She was *like me*. What a relief!

With just one person knowing who I was inside, and how happy that made me, you can imagine how I felt when Yukiko introduced me to her friends Paula, Ariel, and Ella. Suddenly, instead of just two of us in the world—me and Yukiko—there were *five* of us.

The very first time I met Paula, I had a flash that she was Pocahontas. Paula is Native American, with straight dark hair and dark brown eyes. Ariel is red-headed, blue-eyed, impulsive, curious, and fun, fun, fun. Yep—she's the Little Mermaid. Ella is Cinderella, and she even has a stepmother and two stepsisters. (They're not awful, though.)

So there we were: Snow White, Princess Jasmine, Pocahontas, the Little Mermaid, and Cinderella. Five girls whose lives were touched and colored by magic. Five princesses dressed in ordinary clothes. Five Disney Girls that magic had brought together. It was almost like my life started that day. My four new best friends made everything better than it was before. In fact, I decided I definitely wanted to transfer from Greenbriar Academy to Orlando Elementary.

My parents weren't thrilled by that idea, but after six months, I finally convinced them. They let me transfer as long as I kept my grades high, took ballet lessons, went to church with them on Sundays, and didn't start acting like a "hooligan." (I had to look that word up in the dictionary.)

So third grade was the best, going to Orlando Elementary with my new fabulous friends. But guess what. There was still something missing. I know what you're thinking: Isn't that girl ever satisfied? But the thing was, Paula and Ariel are *best* best friends, and so are Ella and Yukiko. And then there was me. Although I loved the other four Disney Girls, and they were my best friends, still, I was dying for a *best* best friend of my very own.

Then, last September, Isabelle transferred to OE from another public school. I took one look at her and knew she was special. Isabelle was super-smart, interesting, and fun. We liked so many of the same things! She loved the Honeygirls. We liked the same clothes. But . . . would she understand about my being a Disney Girl? Would I have to choose between her and my four best friends?

No! Because Isabelle is Belle, from *Beauty and the Beast*! Yes. That is how magic works in my life. It was magic that helped me meet the five people in the world who can understand the real, magical Jasmine underneath. And one of them turned out to be my very own *best*, best friend.

"J?" whispered Isabelle in the dark.

I turned to her. "Are you still awake?"

"Yeah. I couldn't sleep, knowing how upset you were."

See? *Best*, best friends.

"Thanks," I whispered.

"Listen," she said softly. "We'll think of something to get you out of this, okay? The six of us together. We'll work something out—we always do."

I let out a deep breath. "Okay. Thanks." Suddenly I felt very, very tired, and I closed my eyes.

Chapter Five

Rajah in Trouble

"So Paula says to take a big scrap of carpet and hang it on the wall," I explained to Isabelle on Saturday afternoon. I leaned into my closet and pulled out another dress. I held it up. It was too short. I put it in the discard pile. "Then he'll sharpen his claws on it instead of Mother's new fiber sculptures."

Isabelle grinned at me. Her eyes told me she thought the idea of Rajah shredding that sculpture was pretty funny. I grinned back.

"Okay, this has to go," I said, adding a sweater to the

discard pile. A couple times a year, I go through all my clothes and get rid of stuff I don't wear. I give it all to a used clothing store, since I don't have sisters to pass it on to.

Isabelle got up and changed the CD on my boom box. "Listen to this," she said. "It's from the Honeygirls' first album."

I started to sort through the keepers I had piled on my special rug. (It's a small, very old, very magical Persian rug. Luckily, Mother lets me have it in my room even though it doesn't exactly match the rest of my décor.)

"I never thought you'd leave," sang the lead singer of Honeygirls. "Never thought we'd be apart. But now you're gone, my life's gone wrong, and there's ice inside my heart. . . ."

I stared at Isabelle. "Maybe we should play something lighter," I said, and started to fold a T-shirt.

"But it's how I feel," Isabelle said.

I jumped up and put on a bouncy dance tune by Ninja Woman, who's my second-favorite group. I mean, there's the Honeygirls, who are goddesses, and there's Ninja Woman, who are great to listen to in the car, or when you need to be high-energy, and then there's the Casey

Brothers, who are good when neither the Honeygirls nor Ninja Woman is quite right. Between those three bands, I've got just about all my musical needs covered.

Isabelle couldn't help smiling when "Ninja Bopstyle" started playing. That song always does that for me.

"Okay," said Isabelle. "Maybe you're right. But let's get down to business. First, have you tried just telling your parents how you feel about St. John's?"

"Uh huh," I said. "But Daddy doesn't want to get between me and Mother. And Mother thinks that I'm not giving the whole idea of St. John's a fair chance."

"Hmm," said Isabelle. "I was trying to think of what I would do if it were me. I don't know if I would just throw myself down on the floor crying and begging or what. I can't believe that your parents would just send you away, when you don't want to go at all."

When she put it that way, I felt extra terrible. Were Mother and Daddy trying to send me away? They *said* they wanted me to have the best education they could afford. Mother said she wanted me to do all the fun, wonderful things that she had done at St. John's. But did they just want me out of the house?

I moaned and dropped my head into my hands. Just

then, as if he had sensed how unhappy I was (I think pets can be psychic sometimes), Rajah uncoiled from his favorite spot on the window seat and leaped to the floor.

"Whoa," Isabelle laughed. "Was that an earthquake?"

I made a face at her as my little orange baby padded over to me. I patted my stomach, and Rajah jumped up on me, the way he's always done since I first got him.

"Oof!" I said in surprise as he knocked the breath out of my lungs. I couldn't believe it, but I felt almost uncomfortable with him lying on me. It felt like . . . sack of rice, weighing me down. A *big* sack of rice.

Rajah coiled up on my stomach and settled his triangular orange head onto his big paws. His eyes drifted closed. I couldn't help noticing that he was sort of *spilling* off me on all sides. "Gee, I remember when I first got him, he could curl up on my lap, no problem."

Isabelle giggled and rolled her eyes. "He's humongous," she informed me. I squinted and looked at Rajah again. Was he really?

Someone knocked on my door, and Mother came in with a vase of fresh flowers. (Mother loves to have fresh flowers all over the house.)

"Hello, Isabelle, dear," she said, placing the vase on my

dresser. She stepped back and carefully pushed stems here and there until the arrangement looked perfect.

"Hello, Mrs. Prentiss," said Isabelle.

"Are you two discussing St. John's?" Mother asked.

"Uh huh," I said glumly.

"Well, what do you think of boarding schools, Isabelle?" Mother asked. "I remember your mother telling me how much she loved Rosedale."

My eyes opened wide. "Did your mom go to boarding school?"

"Yes," Isabelle admitted.

"You never told me," I said. "You've never even mentioned it."

Isabelle shrugged uncomfortably. "It never came up."

"Rosedale is a lovely school," Mother said brightly.

"Mom only went to Rosedale because the local schools in Kingston weren't very good," Isabelle said. (Isabelle's mom was born in Kingston, Jamaica.)

"But she loved it, didn't she?" persisted Mother.

"Yes, but she *wanted* to go," said Isabelle.

During this talk, Rajah had slithered off my chest and stalked out of the room. He probably felt like we were disturbing his nap.

"Maybe Jasmine should talk to your mother about Rosedale, and her boarding school experiences," suggested Mother.

Isabelle looked trapped. "Ah, okay," she said reluctantly.

"After all, I'm sure you want what's best for Jasmine," Mother continued. "In the long run."

"Uh . . ." Isabelle stammered, gazing at the ground.

"Even if it seems difficult in the short run," said Mother.

Have you ever seen a pretty, blond, feminine bulldozer? That's my mom.

We were saved from this by Rajah, who trotted back into my room with something kind of fuzzy and pale in his mouth. For a horrifying instant, I thought he had found a cream-colored bunny rabbit somewhere. (We don't have rabbits anywhere around us. But I wasn't thinking clearly.)

"Heavens, what's that?" said Mother, looking alarmed.

Rajah proudly came up to me and dropped the wad at my feet. I prepared myself to be majorly grossed out, but when I peeked at the thing, it started to look familiar.

"Oh, geez," I said, poking the filmy lump with my foot. "It's a pair of pantyhose." I started laughing.

"Pantyhose?" Mother frowned. Then her face cleared with recognition. "Oh, no!" she cried. "Those are my new designer pantyhose!" She snatched them up and examined them. Rajah casually licked his paw.

"They're ruined! Ruined!" Mother said. She shook them out to show me how shredded they were. "Jasmine Prentiss, these stockings cost seventeen dollars! I hadn't worn them once yet!" She frowned at me. "We have to do something about that cat, miss, and *soon*." Mother hurried out of my room and shut the door firmly after her.

"I hate it when she calls me miss," I sighed.

Then a terrible thought hit me: what would happen to Rajah once I was gone?

Chapter Six

The End of Magic?

On Sunday, Paula and I had signed up to wash cars at a fund-raiser for our dojo. We spent the whole hot, sunny morning getting soaking and sudsy in the parking lot in front of our karate studio. It was hard work, but also a lot of fun. We were trying to raise money for a new heavy bag for our class. (A heavy bag is a huge punching bag filled with water. It hangs from the ceiling, and we punch it as hard as we can. It's sooo fun.)

In the afternoon the Disney Girls got together at my house. Were we by my pool? Of course.

Isabelle coasted across my pool on my inflatable shark raft. She raised her head a little and took a sip of her iced herb tea.

Usually when we're in my pool, we're doing special DG things—imagination games and pretend stuff that only we would understand. Like sometimes we pretend we're all mermaids living in King Triton's kingdom, and we make up complicated stories and act them out. But today we were too upset about my boarding school to concentrate.

Ella wiped off her sticky hands. "Okay, our first list didn't get us anywhere," she said. "So instead of making a list about how to get Jasmine out of going to St. John's, let's make a list of reasons why Jasmine *shouldn't* go to St. John's."

"I'm going to miss Ella's organizing," I said wistfully.

Ariel pushed her sunglasses up on her nose. "You're not going to miss anything," she said. "You're not going, and that's that. Look at this."

She pulled a somewhat crumpled piece of paper out of her pool bag and proudly passed it around. On it was a message made by cutting out letters from magazines and pasting them together. It said:

35

Your Kid ISN'T welcome AT St. John's keep her home OR else

I groaned when I read it.

"What?" Ariel demanded. "It's brilliant. See, I made it sound like there were people at the *school* who didn't want you there. That way no one would ever suspect that it was us who sent the note."

I turned the paper over. "Except that you used your 'Ariel' stationery," I pointed out. "That might give them a clue."

"Oh." Ariel frowned. "I could make a new one. I could—"

"Thanks, Ariel," I said gently. "It was a good idea. But I just don't think it'll work."

"We have to attack the problem logically," Ella insisted. "First, let's write down your parents' reasons for wanting to send you there. Then we'll destroy each reason, one by one."

"That's a good plan," Paula said. "And maybe we should sit in a circle. You know."

We all knew what she meant, and we scrambled over to a shady spot and sat down. I told you a little bit about our

36

magic before, but there's actually a lot more to it than that. The thing is, the six of us are touched by magic. Magic is in our lives; it's part of who we are and what we do. Each of us felt that way before we even met the others. Now that we're all tight, it's stronger than ever. And we had found out that when the six of us are together, especially if we're in a circle, linking pinkies, our magic seems extra powerful.

After we checked to make sure no one was watching, we linked pinkies and chanted quietly:

"All the magic powers that be,
Hear us now, our special plea.
The six of us can't be apart,
Please help us know where we should start."

For a few moments we sat quietly, our eyes closed, concentrating. Then Paula said, "Jasmine?"

I opened my eyes and said, "Okay. What if my magic, our magic, is somehow centered around being *here*? And what if my leaving here means my magic is weaker—or not there at all? I feel like if I go to St. John's, I might lose who I am!"

My five best friends were quiet for a while.

Isabelle reached out and patted my arm. "The magic is inside you," she said quietly. "You'll take it with you wherever you go."

"Now, why exactly do your parents want you to go?" asked Yukiko.

I ticked the reasons off on my fingers. "They want me to have a better education. They want me to meet kids whose parents are like my parents. All the girls in my family go, and they want to keep doing that tradition. They think St. John's offers better opportunities than a public school in Orlando."

My friends met my eyes. They looked unsure.

"Does St. John's have ballet?" asked Yukiko.

I nodded.

"Does it have karate?" Paula asked.

"No. But it has horseback riding, field hockey, and croquet," I answered. "Not to mention field trips to New York, summers in Europe, the best teachers . . ."

"I love croquet," said Ariel. Ella rolled her eyes.

"Fine. *You* go," I told Ariel.

"Your mom asked if I wanted what was best for you," said Isabelle. "And of course I do. You know I would give anything for you to stay—but what if going to St. John's really is the best thing for you?" She looked as if she was about to cry. "How can I try to convince you to leave us? How could I say good-bye to my best friend? But if I am really am your best friend, I don't want to be selfish. I don't want you to stay when it's better that you go."

Isabelle sniffled and brushed her arm across her eyes. I felt terrible. A tear ran down Yukiko's face.

"I know how Isabelle feels," said Paula. "We probably all do." Ella, Ariel, and Yukiko nodded. "We would never want to stand in your way, if you have a great opportunity. But now that the six of us have found each other, it seems awful to split us up." She shook her head. "I like to be fair about things. But I just can't be fair about this— not when it means you'll be gone for months at a time."

We sat in our sad, silent circle for a long time. In my heart, I knew I would have to say good-bye to them in just seven weeks.

Chapter Seven

St. John's Is So Peachy

I am usually a very upbeat person. There are so many great things in my life, and I actually notice them and am happy about them. I mean, I'm healthy, I have great parents (in general—they were losing serious points over this boarding school thing), I have the best friends in the world, I have a nice place to live, I have a great cat . . . I could go on and on.

But the idea of leaving my whole life to live the life my mom wanted me to, somewhere *else*, was really rocking my world.

Then on Tuesday my mom had a surprise for me.

"Guess what, darling," she said cheerfully at breakfast. "I've decided that it would be a good idea for you to see St. John's in person. So we're going to fly up there this morning and have a good look around." She took a small bite of toast and chewed delicately.

My jaw dropped open. "We're going to St. John's *today*?" I practically shrieked.

"Yes, dear. Just for the day. Daddy's lending us the company plane." Mother looked over at my tank top and carpenter shorts. Her nose wrinkled a tiny bit. "Maybe you should wear something . . ."

"Else?" I supplied.

"Yes, darling. Thank you."

Don't get all excited about my dad having a company plane. It isn't like a jumbo jet or anything. I mean, it's a jet, but just a very small baby jet. That morning Mother and I shared a ride with two of Daddy's coworkers who had to go to South Carolina also.

During the plane ride, Mother did crossword puzzles while I peered out my window. This whole trip seemed so Jasminey to me. I mean, the main Princess Jasmine thing is over-protective parents. When you're an only child, I think your parents sort of spend more time worrying about *you* and trying to take care of *you* and trying to do everything that's best for *you*. But when you have siblings, they don't have as much time to spend on each child. Which is both a good thing and a bad thing. Like, Yukiko has six brothers and one sister. So sometimes Yukiko complains that her parents don't have too much time to spend just hanging out with her and paying attention to every little thing she does. But on the other hand, Yukiko has more freedom than I do, because her parents just don't have the time or energy to worry about whether she should read this book or that book or go on this field trip or wear this dress or whatever.

My parents have the time and the energy. Sometimes it gets in my way, even though I know they mean well.

Now they wanted to send me off to boarding school. A fenced, gated boarding school in a small town in South Carolina. There would be a whole army of teachers and counselors and advisers and student aides to keep an eye on me and help me and work with me and . . . continue over-protecting me.

I sighed as the plane touched down. A dark blue limo

was waiting for Mother and me. I settled back against the seat and smoothed my skirt nicely. Inside I felt like crying.

Mother pressed the button that lowered her window. She breathed happily. "Smell the air, Jazzy," she said. "It's so different here than it is in Florida."

I sniffed and nodded. This is why I love traveling, usually. Today I was bummed because I didn't want to see St. John's, but if it weren't for that, I would be totally into today's trip. I love seeing new places, new people, new everything. Did you know that the water tastes different everywhere? Each place has its own special water taste. Each place has its own air smell. People speak with different accents (or different languages), wear different clothes, drive different cars. It's so interesting! I wish I could see every single town, city, and village in the entire world! Maybe I will someday. Today, I was seeing South Carolina.

Half an hour later our driver stopped at some tall stone gates that looked as if they had been shipped here from England. A voice buzzed him through. I looked around— I couldn't help being interested.

St. John's was really, really pretty. Even I had to admit

that. One thing about Florida: it's extremely flat. Flat, flat, flat. And mostly there are pine trees, and some live oaks, pecans, magnolias, and cypresses. In South Carolina there are beautiful, gentle hills, covered with thick green grass and all kinds of pretty trees, like maples, sycamores, tuliptrees, and dogwoods. There's more variety than in Florida.

The driver pulled up in front of the main building, which was made out of grayish-brown stone. A tall, well-dressed black woman walked gracefully down the steps and held a hand out to Mother.

"Hello, and welcome to St. John's," she said pleasantly. "I'm Helen Chambers, and I'd love to show you both around today."

"Oh, thank you, Helen," said Mother, smiling. I smiled too, to be polite. I could tell my mom was so happy to be here, where she'd had such good experiences. And Helen seemed just like the kind of person my mom is most comfortable with. They were already talking as if they were old friends.

I looked down at my white sandals tapping against the flagstones. Mother was sure I would be as happy here as she had been. But how could I?

Chapter Eight

Make Your Pet a Star

Mother and I returned home late Tuesday night. The next day, Isabelle had to visit her cousins in the morning. After a bunch of phone calls, the DGs agreed to meet at Lakeview Mall at three o'clock.

I got there first and sat on the bench by the fountain in the middle. Isabelle was next to rush up.

"I want to hear all about it!" she said breathlessly. "Yesterday seemed to last forever! But also, guess what? My favorite author is at the bookstore here, signing copies of her latest book! Do you think we could go there?"

"Yeah, sure," I said. "That'll be so cool."

Ariel was the last to arrive, of course. She's late so often that we usually tell her to show up half an hour before the rest of us are due to get there.

We snagged a table in the food court and got snacks and drinks. (The vegetarian burrito at Los Pecos is awesome.)

I told them all about St. John's. How pretty it was, how cool the teachers had been, how fabulous all their resources were. I told Paula and Ariel about the incredible gym, and Isabelle about the full-time poetry teacher. Some students had been at St. John's, doing summer programs, and I told Ella and Yukiko how nice the kids had seemed. The summer programs had been in everything from horseback-riding to math workshops to sewing to computer skills.

"So it was fabulous," said Paula, summing it up.

I sighed. "Yep. So how about it? Did you guys ask your parents?" The five of them nodded. They had agreed to ask their folks if there was any way they could join me at St. John's. It was about as likely as an honest snake-charmer, but we'd decided to try.

"Mom says I'm lucky to have a good public school right

here," said Isabelle. "She didn't buy the whole St. John's thing at all. Despite Rosedale."

"My dad said there's no way we could afford it," said Ella.

"Me neither," said Paula. "Mom's got to pay off all her school loans." Vet school was expensive.

"I think we can afford it," said Yukiko, "but I have to tell you—I just didn't think I could go."

"What did your parents say?" I asked.

Yukiko blushed. "I mean, I just didn't think *I* could go. *Me*. I thought about it and thought about it, but in the end I knew I would just be miserable being away from everyone. I mean, I know the Dwarfs make me totally crazy sometimes, but I don't want to live hundreds of miles away from them. I just don't."

"I don't want to live hundreds of miles away, either," I said sadly. "But it looks like I don't have much choice. Mother signed me up for the fall semester while we were up there." I reached over and patted Yukiko's arm. "It's okay. I understand. It was a dumb idea, anyway."

Somehow I managed to down the rest of my burrito, even though I totally wasn't into it anymore. My friends looked sad. I looked sad too. I was giving everyone the mopes.

"Hey, Isabelle," I said, sitting up straighter. "We better get to Bookends, while your author is still there."

Isabelle looked up at me.

"Come on," I ordered. I stood up and gathered my trash. "Let's go."

Of course, Isabelle was totally thrilled to actually meet the author of *The Elf Wars* trilogy, one of her all-time favorite series. After we left the bookstore, she kept staring at the author's autograph, and her face was shining. I felt happy to see her so happy. That's one of the coolest parts about being *best* best friends—anything your *best* best friend feels, you feel too. Like you're connected.

Anyway, we were walking through the mall, sort of window shopping and hanging out. We had to stop like every twenty seconds so Ariel could look at cute shoes or something. All of a sudden, I saw a sign right ahead of me. It was like magic had put it there, just for me to notice.

The sign said, MAKE YOUR PET A STAR!

"Guys, guys!" I said excitedly. "Check this out!" I dragged my friends over to the billboard.

Quickly I skimmed the info. The billboard was from

the "America's Wackiest Pets" TV show. They were looking for video tapes of people's pets doing funny things. This season's winner would get ten thousand dollars and a year's supply of pet food.

"Oh, my gosh!" I cried. "This is perfect! If I enter Rajah, and he wins, my parents will think he's fabulous!"

"Hmm—we've got only a week until the deadline," Paula read. She looked up and smiled. "This could be really fun. I wonder if I could catch Meeko doing something weird."

Yes, Paula really does have a real, live raccoon named Meeko. Basically, he's the most heinous pet on the entire planet.

"I don't know, Paula," Ariel said thoughtfully. "I mean, catch Meeko doing something weird? You might actually have to, like, be in the same room with him, with a video camera, for about four seconds."

Paula grinned and punched Ariel lightly on her arm.

"This is it!" I crowed. "This is going to save Rajah's reputation! I'm going to make my pet a star!"

Chapter Nine

America's Most Boring Pet

Guess what. Rajah was not a kitten anymore.

I realized this after I had followed him around for two days straight with our video camera. When he was a kitten, Rajah had done something awesomely cute about every five minutes. He had played with toys, he had hidden under things and leaped out at people, he had tried to climb tall things . . . He had been just the most incredibly adorable thing in the whole history of kitten-dom. He had been marmalade colored, with a pointy, fuzzy tail, big blue eyes, and sharp, triangular ears that looked too large for his sweet little head. He had said, "Mew! Mew!" in a high kitteny voice.

After two days of closely watching him, I had to admit that my darling baby had gone through some changes. For one thing, I couldn't pick him up with one hand anymore. I had to use two hands, and I had to bend my knees first so I wouldn't strain my back. For another thing, he wasn't so much cute as really handsome. His eyes had changed to a deep golden color, like maple syrup. He had gotten bigger all over, so his paws and ears and tail all looked the right size. His fur was thicker and silkier and lay flatter, so he didn't look like a little fuzzball anymore.

But the main clue I had that he was grown up was that pretty much all he did was eat and sleep and sleep and maybe eat a little and then take a nap before dinnertime. I got tons of footage of him looking gorgeous and regal and majestic. But interesting? Nada.

"I mean, probably no one would pay ten-thousand dollars for a video of an incredibly good-looking cat washing himself, or stretching, right?" I asked my parents that night at dinner.

"I shouldn't think so, darling," said Daddy, touching

his napkin to his lips. (Daddy is from England. That's why he talks funny.)

"Not unless they were soft in the head," Mother agreed, helping herself to asparagus soufflé. "Have you been able to catch him in the act of destroying something? That shouldn't be too hard, I'd imagine, and it would at least be more interesting."

Mother and Daddy smiled at each other. They think the same kinds of things are funny, even though she's young and American, and he's much older and English.

"Oh, ha ha," I said, making a face at Mother. She giggled.

"I mean, Paula already has like five different things on video," I complained. "Practically everyone's pets are more interesting than Rajah." I felt a teensy bit guilty putting Rajah down like that. Just because he was kind of boring didn't mean I didn't totally adore him and love him to pieces. It just meant I had to face the fact that he wasn't America's Wackiest Pet material.

"What sorts of things does Paula have captured on videotape?" Daddy asked.

"Well, Bobby, you know, her beagle that has only three legs? He was chasing a squirrel and it ran right up their little persimmon tree and Bobby followed it and of course dogs don't climb trees so he got totally stuck and was sitting on a branch howling and the squirrel was way up high scolding him and throwing rotten persimmons at him. And Paula was there with her camera!"

My parents laughed. "Poor dog," said Daddy.

"And then that night, after dinner, Meeko got into a box of cornstarch and spilled it all over everything and played in it so he was completely covered with it. Then he ran through the living room, and Paula's Great-Uncle Happy was there. He's very superstitious, and he thought it was like the ghost of a raccoon and he sort of freaked out."

"Paula filmed that?" Daddy said admiringly.

I nodded. "She just grabbed her camera, and boom."

"What luck," Mother said.

"That's not all. Last week Ella's pet mice escaped from their cage, and I guess they could smell the outdoors or something from the mail slot on the front door, so they climbed up the front door and were just poking their noses through the slot when the mail carrier came and started to put the letters through, and then she saw these mouse noses coming at her and she screamed and threw all the mail up into the air and leaped backwards and almost fell off their porch and practically brought a lawsuit against the O'Connors. But Ella didn't videotape any of it."

Mother and Daddy were laughing so hard they couldn't even speak. I felt happy. I love making them laugh and having them pay attention to me. I mean, they always pay attention to me, but I like it when I'm like the star.

All of a sudden I realized how much I would miss my parents if I was away at a boarding school. I would miss being in my room at night, and knowing they were just down the hall, or hearing them speaking in the library while I was doing my homework, or curling up with Mother on her bed to watch Martha Stewart on TV, or some movie by Jane Austen or something. Did Daddy realize how much he would miss me if I wasn't here to play croquet with him, or tennis? Would Mother miss me? What were they *thinking*?

"Darling?" Mother began, looking at my face.

I was about to explain how I felt, but just then Rajah decided to do something interesting.

With no warning, my huge orange cat jumped up *onto* the dining room table, where he is absolutely forbidden.

"Rajah!" I cried.

"Shoo!" Mother said, waving her napkin at him.

Then Rajah hunched up, coughed, and *barfed* right next to my *plate*! On the lace tablecloth. By the Limoges serving bowl of mushroom soup.

I gasped. I had never seen anything so incredibly gross in my entire life. My parents both yelped and leaped up away from the table.

"Mrs. Perth!" Mother called loudly. "Mrs. Perth!"

I scooped Rajah up in my arms, praying that he was done barfing. As fast as I could, I carried him through the kitchen and set him down in the mud room. I stroked his back, but kept on my feet in case he barfed again and I had to jump out of the way.

"What's wrong, baby? Did you eat something bad?" I asked.

I could still hear the commotion going on in the dining room. I knew that my little tummy-ache guy had just gone waaay down in his popularity ratings with my parents. Bummer.

And the worst thing, of course, was that I hadn't been anywhere *near* my video camera.

Chapter Ten

What To Take?

Rajah hid most of the day on Monday. He was incredibly embarrassed. I couldn't blame him. If I had suddenly thrown up on someone's dining room table, I would just want to sink beneath the face of the earth.

In the afternoon, my friends got rides over to my house. We went swimming for a while, then ate lunch by the pool. Mrs. Perth fixed us all hot dogs, except for Paula, who had a peanut-butter sandwich.

"How was ballet this morning?" asked Isabelle.

"Cool," I said. "They're starting to audition for parts

for the end-of-summer recital. I guess I'll still be here for that."

My friends gave me sympathetic looks.

"I'm going to try out for the part of a surfer," said Yukiko.

"A ballerina surfer?" Ella giggled.

Yukiko grinned. "It's going to be pretty funky. Not like at Christmas, when we do the *Nutcracker*. That's always really traditional. The summer show is usually experimental and modern."

"That sounds awesome," said Ariel. She frowned. "I wonder if I—"

"No!" we all shouted at the same time. Last fall, Ariel had decided she just had to be in the ballet recital at Madame Pavlova's. Let's just say that we're glad she realized that swimming is her best sport.

I sat up. "You guys want to head in for a while? I'm kind of waterlogged."

Once we had changed into regular clothes, we hung out in my room, listening to tunes. Paula had a new CD by one of her favorite singers, Melody Bluestar. It was kind of new agey and pretty.

"Oh, wow, I almost forgot!" said Yukiko. She dug

around in her fanny pack and pulled out a newspaper clipping. "I meant to show this to you guys earlier. Look!"

We crowded around and read the clipping. It was from today's newspaper, and it was advertising a . . .

"Pet show!" I exclaimed, reading it excitedly. "A local pet show, right at the mall! It's on July Fourth weekend."

"Let me see it," Paula asked.

"Any pet can enter," Isabelle read. She looked up, her brown eyes shining. "Any pet like, Rajah, for instance?"

"Or Meeko," said Paula.

"Or Jaq and Gus," Ella said.

Yukiko made a delicate snorting sound. "Ella, what category could Jaq and Gus win? Most Rodentlike?"

"Hey, they're very cute," Ella protested.

"Come on," I said. "I'll go make copies of the entry form on Daddy's copier. Then we can all fax them in. We can pay the five-dollar entrance fee the day of the show. This will be so cool!"

So I entered Rajah in the "Most Beautiful Cat" category. Paula entered Meeko in the "Most Unusual Pet" category. (Paula has a bunch of other pets, too, but she thought her raccoon was probably the most unusual.) Ella decided not to enter her mice. Yukiko didn't want to enter any of her four cats, and Isabelle's two dogs didn't really fit any category. Ariel has only fish (big surprise), and she couldn't figure out how to get them to the mall. (Thank goodness.)

After we faxed in our forms, I flopped down on my bean bag chair. "This will do it," I said. "If Rajah wins some kind of trophy, my parents just might forgive him for the dining room incident."

"What about the forty-nine other incidents he's had lately?" asked Isabelle.

I looked around for something to throw at her, and she laughed. Then it hit me again: how much I was going to miss all of them. My face sobered.

"You know, I guess I better start thinking about what I'm going to take with me to St. John's," I said.

The mood of the room plunged about a hundred and fifty degrees. Five pairs of sad DG eyes looked my way.

"Don't talk about it," Ariel said grumpily.

I stood up and looked, really looked, at the stuff in my room. Most of the big things in my room were my mom's choices. But most of the little things were mine.

"I can take one large trunk of stuff," I told my friends.

"Plus two big suitcases, and two cardboard boxes of books and music."

"Can I fit into one of the suitcases?" Isabelle asked shakily. I went over and gave her a hug.

"We'll have to do magic-wish conference calls," I tried to joke. My friends sat silently around my room. As I walked around, so many wonderful memories came back to me. I decided to take my special magic rug and my favorite pillow.

"Oh, I *have* to take this," I said, picking up a framed photograph. I held it up so all my friends could see. It was a picture of the six of us that my mom had taken last spring at Walt Disney World. All of us DGs had spent a magical week together at the Disney Institute. Mother had taken this picture the last day. We were all standing in a line, our arms around each other and huge smiles on our faces. Whenever I looked at the picture, I could see a special glow of magic floating around us. To me, this picture summed up everything that we are to each other. I had made copies and given each of my best friends one.

Then I heard a sniff, and when I looked up, Isabelle was crying. I ran over to her and put my arm around her again.

"Don't cry," I said, trying to be brave. "It'll be okay."

"I looked in my mirror last night," Isabelle said, in between sobs. "And I saw you here, in your own room, getting ready for school in the fall. And I knew it wasn't true! I knew you would be in a strange place, instead! I felt like my magic had let me down." She threw herself down on my bed and cried into my pillow.

(You remember—Belle has a magic mirror that lets her see things. Isabelle really does have a tiny one, a charm that she wears. Her magic lets her see things in it.)

"Maybe without you, all of our magic will be weaker," said Ella in a worried voice.

"I don't think so," Paula said reassuringly, but her face looked concerned.

"Paula, I've been thinking," I said solemnly. "I know my parents would let Rajah stay here while I'm gone. But I think he would be happier with people who actually liked him. I was wondering—do you think your parents would let Rajah live with you? I would take him back during holidays."

Paula's dark brown eyes opened wider, then her whole face crumpled, and she burst into tears. Paula doesn't cry very often, so I was pretty shocked. Next thing I knew, I was crying, Ella was crying, Yukiko was crying, and Ariel was bawling her lungs out. Instead of the usual glowy halo of magic that surrounds us when we're together, there was a dark, threatening cloud hovering over our heads.

I didn't even hear my mom knock on my door. But suddenly she was there, in the open doorway, staring at us in alarm.

"We don't want her to go!" Ariel sobbed, covering her eyes.

Mother looked so crushed and disappointed. I tried to stop crying, but my chest hurt and I had to let some of the pain out.

Mother came and knelt next to me. She reached up and handed Paula and Ariel tissues, then stroked my hair. "Darling, I'm so sorry you feel unhappy about this," she murmured. "I'm surprised you feel this way. I was thrilled and excited when it was my turn to go to St. John's. I begged my mother to let me start early. I don't know what to say."

I put my head on her shoulder and cried.

"I just know that once you get there, you'll have such an amazing time," said Mother. "You'll have these wonderful friends at home, and you'll also have wonderful new friends at school."

I cried some more. Finally, looking sad, Mother sighed and tiptoed out.

Chapter Eleven

So Brilliant

"I hate to tell you this, Jasmine," said Ariel.

"But you're going to tell me anyway," I guessed.

"Yes. This is the most boring video I have ever seen in my entire life," Ariel stated.

It was Tuesday, the day after the sob-fest. We were all at Ella's house, in her family room. This morning we had all spent a couple hours working in her room. Lots of old wallpaper needed to be scraped off the walls before Ella and her stepmom, Alana, could put up the new wallpaper Ella had chosen.

Scraping wallpaper was hard work. We had decided to take a break before Paula and I had to head to the dojo for our four o'clock tae kwan do class.

"I have to agree with Ariel," said Yukiko. "And I've seen some boring videos. Like my cousin's wedding. Now *that* was a boring tape."

Okay. What was so boring? What were my friends complaining about? It was my "America's Wackiest Pets" video of Rajah. Even my very best friend in the entire world, Isabelle, was starting to look a little twitchy.

"How many times do we have to watch this cat wash himself?" Ella grumbled, resting her chin on her hand.

"Jasmine," Isabelle said gently, "once you saw that Rajah was sleeping like he was in a coma, why did you *keep on filming*?"

I sighed. "I was hoping he would wake up."

"Yeah, and do something interesting. Like wash himself," grumbled Ariel.

"Okay, okay!" I said, jumping to my feet. "So you don't want to watch two hours of my cat doing nothing. I get the message." I picked up the remote and pointed it at the VCR. But before I clicked the off button, in the background of the video, we saw my mom approach the camera, a fabric swatch in her hand. "Jazzy, what do you think of this curtain material?" her voice asked.

My own voice, sounding muffled, answered, "Later. Mother, could you sort of poke Rajah with your foot, and try to wake him up a little?" Then you could hear my mom laughing.

I froze. Then I hit the rewind button.

"Oh, no!" cried Yukiko. "Not again!"

"Just a sec," I commanded, searching for a certain spot on the tape. "Here! Here," I muttered, clicking Play.

"I think it's snack time," said Ella, starting to get up. The image of Rajah sprawled asleep on my windowseat, his big head hanging off of it, upside down, popped up on the screen.

"Um, can I show you guys my video of Meeko trying to make his own peanut-butter sandwich?" asked Paula.

"Wait—" I said, staring at the screen. In the background of the video, you could see my dad come to the door of my room. "Hurry, Jasmine," he said. "We want to try that new seafood place out by the lake. A family luncheon out."

Slowly, an idea started to take shape inside my brain. I quickly replayed a couple more scenes.

"Jasmine, you think—" said Isabelle, frowning in concentration.

I shivered as a quick burst of magic made the air crackle around me. I looked up and met Isabelle's eyes. She held out her arm, and showed me goosebumps.

"This is it!" I cried, throwing the remote in the air.

"Yes!" cried Isabelle, jumping up and grabbing my hands. We spun in a circle together.

"I've got it," Paula said slowly.

"I see it too," said Ella in wonder.

"I can't believe we didn't think of it before," said Ariel.

I nudged her with my foot. "If you hadn't been so busy complaining about my cat, you would have noticed it!" I teased her.

If you're wondering what was going on, I can tell you: the six of us, plus magic, plus my videotape of Rajah, had come up with the solution to the biggest problem of my entire life: how not to go to St. John's.

We immediately huddled in a circle, and started to work out the details of our plan.

Chapter Twelve

This Is Your Life

Even with all of us working together, it still took almost two weeks to get our plan ready. After all, we couldn't spend all day, every day on it. Each of us had tons of activities and other stuff to do on top of my big plan.

So with everything else going on, it was practically August before we could set a date for the presentation. It was now or never: Mother and Daddy were going to Belgium for four days on Friday, and I definitely wanted to have St. John's wrapped up before then.

For the big event, we picked Wednesday night, right

after dinner. When Disney Girls started ringing our door-bell, Mother looked mystified. "Are you having a sleep-over, darling?" she asked. She pulled out her pocket organizer and clicked a few buttons. "I don't have it in my schedule."

I shook my head as Mrs. Perth let Isabelle, Paula, and Ariel into the foyer. "This is just a quick get-together," I explained. "And I want you and Daddy to be there. Can you meet us in the family room in ten minutes?"

Mother raised one eyebrow and nodded. I could tell she was wondering what this was all about. She was probably hoping that we wouldn't all start bawling again.

Ten minutes later, we gathered in my family room. We had each taken a section of our project, and we each had a script to read from. Of course, I had to start first.

I seated Mother and Daddy on the sofa, facing our big TV. Standing at the front of the room, I cleared my throat nervously. I tried not to read from my script too much. I wanted to express what I was truly feeling.

"Mother, Daddy," I began. "I know you guys have your hearts set on my going to St. John's. And I understand most of your reasons for wanting me to go. Before we begin tonight, I want to tell you that I appreciate your wanting to do what's best for me. And how you're willing to spend tons of money on my schooling.

"You know I'm not happy about going to St. John's, but you might think it's just because I don't want to leave my friends. And that's definitely a big reason. But I have some other reasons, too, that are just as important. And I wanted to tell you about them."

I nodded to Isabelle, and she took her place in front of my parents. She looked tense.

"Ahem. Education is one of the most important things a person can have," she began. "A good education can raise a person up and make almost any goal achievable."

My parents nodded. I knew choosing Belle to do the education part had been a good idea.

"But it's also true that the word education can mean more than just schooling," continued Isabelle. She straightened her shoulders and suddenly looked very princesslike and magical. "It can also mean life experiences—the things you learn just by living every day." She nodded at Ella, who began the videotape. The video opened with a shot of Orlando Elementary.

"Orlando Elementary is a public school," Isabelle said.

70

"It doesn't have the resources of St. John's. But it's still a very good school."

We had gone to OE and filmed some of the school's awards hanging in the front hallway. We had also gone to a film-developing place and had them transfer old video of me winning the third-grade history award. Not only that, but Isabelle had researched articles about how Orlando Elementary was one of the top-rated public schools in all of Florida, and how many of its students win national awards, and stuff like that.

"A school is more than a collection of classrooms," Isabelle narrated. "It is a place where friendships are formed, ideas are inspired, and role models are discovered. Jasmine has found all of that at OE." The video showed pictures of class picnics and parties, of third-grade graduation, of me and my friends goofing around, and also pictures of projects I had done in third and fourth grades. We ended with still photographs of my report cards, showing my good grades and positive reports from my teachers.

"St. John's is a terrific school," Isabelle concluded. "But OE is also capable of teaching Jasmine a lot."

I stood up again as Isabelle took her seat. "Of course I'll

miss my friends," I told my parents. "But I'll also miss you, so much! Have you thought about how you're going to miss *me*?"

The video continued with clips from a bunch of home movies: paying croquet with Daddy, horseback riding with Mother. The three of us playing Junior Scrabble and Pictionary and laughing. Our Easter egg hunt, Mother and I in our fancy Easter clothes. Our Christmas trees, our Thanksgiving dinners, our birthday parties. The time Daddy had surprised Mother with a new car. Me opening the box with Rajah in it.

I glanced over at my parents and saw that they were holding hands and Mother was dabbing at her eyes. That was a good sign. I was practically crying myself.

Paula stood up. "Last but not least, there are Jasmine's friends. We know she'll make new friends at St. John's. But we don't know that we could ever find anyone to take Jasmine's place—not in our group, and definitely not in our hearts."

The video showed different clips of Disney Girl stuff— at least, as much as we could show without giving away any DG secrets. It showed us all at the Disney Institute, and at Walt Disney World. It showed us splashing in my pool; dressed up in princess costumes; all of us trying to help Ella make a gingerbread castle for Christmas.

Paula continued, "We need Jasmine here. But more important, we think you need Jasmine here too." She sat down.

My parents looked at each other.

Yukiko took her turn. "We have a lot of traditions in my family. And I think they're a good thing. They help us feel connected. They give us a sense of history, and continuation. But every once in a while, a tradition needs to be looked at again. To make sure it has value in itself, and not just as a tradition."

I stood up again as Ariel started rewinding the video.

"Just please, think about it," I said. Then I took a deep breath, and my friends and I all joined hands. Our presentation was over. Now there was nothing to do but wait for my parents' response—and decision.

Chapter Thirteen

There's No Place Like Home

"Goodness," said Daddy, clearing his throat. "You girls have certainly put a great deal of effort into this."

"It was important to me—to us," I said.

"Um, I need time to think about this," Mother said. "I had my heart set on your attending St. John's in the fall. But now I need to think about everything that you've said tonight."

I nodded, and motioned my friends to join me in the kitchen. Mrs. Perth was in there, waiting with popcorn and lemonade for us. (Mrs. Perth is more than just a housekeeper. She's practically like a live-in grandmother.

She helped take care of Daddy when he was just a little boy, in England.)

"How did it go, gels?" she asked in her thick Scottish accent.

"I don't know," I said helplessly. "I think we said all we could say."

Mrs. Perth gave me a hug. She's very comfortable to hug.

Rajah wandered in and headed for his food bowl.

"Hey, big boy," I said.

"We're still on for Saturday, right?" Paula asked.

"Uh huh," I said. "We're all registered and confirmed for the pet show."

"My mom said she'd give us a ride to the mall in our minivan," Ariel said.

"Great, great," I said absently. My mind was whirling with thoughts and I could hardly concentrate on anything. Isabelle stood right next to me. She didn't have to say anything. I knew what she was thinking, and she knew my thoughts too. By the end of this evening, I would know whether I would be staying with the Disney Girls, living my own life, or heading off to St. John's in a month, to be a princess in exile.

It seemed like about nine hours before Mother and

Daddy came and found us in the kitchen. The clock said it had been only twenty minutes.

When my parents walked in, we all stopped talking and stared at them. I felt shaky all over, and I grabbed onto Isabelle's T-shirt.

Mother and Daddy didn't seem to know where to begin. They glanced at each other, as if willing the other one to start.

Finally, when I was about to break apart into a million hysterical pieces, Daddy cleared his throat.

"Well," he said brightly. "You certainly did give us a lot to talk about, and to think about."

AND??? I wanted to scream.

"Daddy means, that after thinking about it, we've realized that maybe we hadn't considered all the aspects of having you attend St. John's," said Mother. She smiled a little. "I have to admit that I hadn't even thought about how much we'd miss you, and how miserable I would be without my Jazzy." She stepped over to me and ruffled my hair. I turned and hugged her around her waist.

"So we're thinking," said Daddy, "that perhaps we're not quite as ready as we thought we all were to have you head off to St. John's."

My eyes opened wide.

Daddy held up a finger. "This doesn't mean that we won't ever want you to go to St. John's, mind you. It just means that we've thought it over, and decided it would be best if we waited a while—when you're ten, perhaps, or eleven."

"Or twelve," said Mother.

The five Disney Girls and I all stared at each other in amazement. Magic had come through again! Magic had given me the idea of the presentation, and it had worked! Not to mention all the magic wishes we had made. And Isabelle's mirror had been right, after all. I would be here, getting ready for school in the fall. Not in South Carolina. Not this year.

"All right!" Ariel yelled, punching the air.

"Yay!" shouted Isabelle. She and I flew at each other, hugging and jumping up and down. Then the six of us glommed together in a huge group hug.

"I'm staying!" I shrieked. "I'm staying!"

"Together forever!" cried Ella and Yukiko. "Awesome!"

It was a wonderful, magical Disney Girl moment.

Chapter Fourteen

Who's Number One?

The very next day, Mother and Daddy took the company plane to Belgium. They would be back on Monday. The house seemed quieter and empty without them. Instead of staying in the big house by myself (with Mrs. Perth) while they were gone, I had gotten permission to hang at Isabelle's. It was like a four-day sleepover, and it was so, so cool—like being sisters. Sisters who happened to have different parents.

Saturday was another hot, sunny, muggy summer day in Orlando. As usual, it was about ninety-eight degrees by nine o'clock in the morning. Mrs. Ramos and Ariel picked up me and Isabelle first thing in the morning, then we stopped by Paula's house to get her and Meeko. Meeko looked so angry in his cat carrier. He kept swiping his paws through the bars, trying to grab Paula's shirt.

"Hush," she said gently. "Try to take a nap. He's super grumpy because he usually sleeps all day," she reminded us. "I hadn't even thought about how a nocturnal animal would do at a daytime pet show." She made an exaggerated scared face, and we laughed.

The rest of the DGs were waiting for us at their houses. Our last stop was my house, where I managed to push Rajah into the carrier that had seemed so huge for him when he was a kitten.

"Come on, boy," I crooned as he glared at me through the bars. "Let's go show them who's number one."

"Girls?" said Mrs. Ramos. "It's almost dinnertime."

"Mph," Ariel mumbled tiredly. She was slouched across the couch in her family room, one arm draped over her eyes.

The rest of us couldn't even respond.

"I was thinking we could order some pizza," Mrs. Ramos said.

Pizza? I managed to pry one eye open. "That sounds good," I croaked.

"Vegetarian, please," Paula whimpered, not moving from where she lay on the floor.

"Okay," said Mrs. Ramos. "I'll call you when it gets here. You guys had kind of a hard day, huh?"

Several of us grunted softly.

After she left, Ella moaned, "No. It wasn't hard. Unless you count chasing an insane raccoon around an entire mall *hard*."

"I *told* you, I don't know how he escaped," Paula said testily.

"He just undid his cage," Yukiko reminded her. "He's pretty smart."

"Too smart," said Ariel tiredly.

"He did win 'Most Unusual Pet,'" I pointed out, trying to look on the bright side.

"Too bad they weren't giving out awards for 'Most Obnoxious Pet,'" said Ariel.

Paula raised herself up on her elbows. "Look, it wasn't my fau—"

"Guys, come on," I said. "Let's not argue. We've been over this a thousand times. The cage wasn't raccoon proof. It wasn't anyone's fault. It just happened. And Meeko and Rajah both won blue ribbons. Let's just concentrate on that."

Usually Paula is the peacemaker in our group, but she was too wound up right now. Plus, it was her raccoon who had escaped.

"You have to admit," said Isabelle, "it was *most unusual* to see a raccoon disappearing into the Laura Ashley store."

I couldn't help it. Just remembering the sight of Meeko, a fat brown and black striped raccoon, racing beneath shoppers' legs and streaking into the window display of Yukiko's favorite store was enough to make my exhausted face creak into a smile.

"It wasn't funny, Jasmine," said Yukiko. "They'll probably never let me in there again. I mean, when Meeko climbed to the top of that mannequin—"

"And then when he was up on the shelf, throwing napkin rings down at the saleslady who was yelling at him," continued Ella.

"And then when he leaped down, trying to get back to Paula, but that shopper got in the way, and he landed on that table display—" said Isabelle.

"Knocking over the whole display—" said Ariel.

"Well, you do have to admit," I finished. "It was most unusual."

By this time, none of us could keep a straight face. By the time Mrs. Ramos came to tell us the pizzas were here, all she could see was six exhausted, rumpled Disney Girls, rolling helplessly on the floor with hysterical laughter.

When my parents came home on Monday, I was ready for them. Rajah's blue ribbon and certificate for first place were waiting on the dining room table, so they would be sure to notice.

"Darling, what's this?" Mother asked, picking up the blue ribbon.

"Rajah's first place ribbon," I said modestly. "I took him to that pet show at the mall, you know, and the judges were really impressed."

"My, my," said Daddy. "He came in first, eh?" Daddy glanced up to see Rajah sitting in the doorway of the kitchen. Rajah casually lifted one large paw and started washing his face. Daddy cocked his head to one side.

"You know, I suppose he is rather a handsome

animal," he said. "That is, when he isn't vomiting on the table."

"Darling, let's not talk about that," Mother murmured. "First place. That's quite an achievement. How many other cats were there?"

"One hundred and six," I said.

"And Rajah beat all of them?" Mother said.

I shrugged. "First place."

"Was this like the Westminster Kennel Dog Show?" asked Daddy. "Except for cats?"

"It was open to all pets," I answered. "Paula's raccoon Meeko got a first-place ribbon too, for Most Unusual pet." I didn't tell them the rest of the story. Let them read about it in the newspaper.

"Well, I'm impressed, Jazzy, and Rajah," Mother said, including my cat in her smile. "Good for you."

Daddy was peering closely at the ribbon. "What exactly does this say?" he asked, pulling out his glasses. "Is this Best in Show, or something?"

"Something like that," I said vaguely, trying to ease the ribbon out of his hands.

Daddy slipped on his glasses and squinted down at the ribbon. I sighed.

"What's this?" Daddy slowly read the tiny silver letters on the ribbon. "First Place, Grand Prize winner, for . . . Heaviest Cat."

"Heaviest Cat?" my mom repeated, trying to read over his shoulder.

"That's what it says," Daddy announced, straightening. "Jasmine's animal won a prize for being the fattest feline entered in competition."

"Give me that," I said, snatching the ribbon away.

"The most corpulent cat," Daddy went on. "The chubbiest chap they had ever seen."

"Daddy! Stop," I said. "You'll hurt his feelings." I went to Rajah and covered his pointy ears with my hands.

"The plumpest pet," Daddy intoned.

"Darling," giggled Mother.

"The beefiest boy—"

"Okay! Okay!" I cried. "I get the picture! Rajah needs to cut down a little. I get it. Now stop before you give him a complex." I scooped Rajah up in my arms and fled to my room. Behind me, I could hear my parents laughing softly.

I couldn't help smiling. We were all home together—and we would stay that way, thanks to the Disney Girls.

Here's a sneak preview of

Disney Girls

#10 *Princess of Power*

Jasmine and I walked to the center of the sparring mat. We both wore our white karate uniforms and our orange belts knotted around our waists. The room was full of other students, friends, and the Disney Girls. I could feel everyone's eyes on us. It felt so strange to be facing one of my best friends, and knowing that I had to win this match to get my green belt.

What was I doing? Jasmine and I had decided to take karate together for fun. Now here we were, facing each other in a competition. I was used to working with my friends—not against them. The worst thing was, I realized that I really wanted to win. I had been practicing and working out and aiming toward this goal. I didn't want to back down now.

But how did this competition fit in with being best friends—with being Disney Girls? How did it fit in with magic? By trying to meet my goal in karate, was I going to hurt the people I loved most in the world? Then Sensei Kerry stepped forward and touched our hands. "Ready?" she asked. "Begin."

I stepped forward.

Read all the books in the
Disney Girls series!

#1 *One of Us*

Jasmine is thrilled to be a Disney Girl. It means she has four best friends—Ariel, Yukiko, Paula, and Ella. But she still doesn't have a *best* best friend. Then she meets Isabelle Beaumont, the new girl. Maybe Isabelle could be Jasmine's best best friend—but could she be a *Disney Girl*?

#2 *Attack of the Beast*

Isabelle's next-door neighbor Kenny has been a total Beast for as long as she can remember. But now he's gone too far: he secretly videotaped the Disney Girls singing and dancing and acting silly at Isabelle's slumber party. Isabelle vows to get the tape back, but how will she ever get past the Beast?

#3 *And Sleepy Makes Seven*

Mrs. Hayashi is expecting a baby soon, and Yukiko is praying that this time it'll be a girl. She's already got six younger brothers and stepbrothers, and this is her last chance for a sister. All of the Disney Girls are hoping that with a little magic, Yukiko's fondest wish will come true.

#4 *A Fish Out of Water*

Ariel in ballet class? That's like putting a fish in the middle of the desert! Even though Ariel's the star of her swim team, she decides that she wants to spend more time with the other Disney Girls. So she joins Jasmine and Yukiko's ballet class.

But has Ariel made a mistake, or will she trade in her flippers for toe shoes forever?

#5 *Cinderella's Castle*

The Disney Girls are so excited about the school's holiday party. Ella decides that the perfect thing for her to make is an elaborate gingerbread castle. But creating such a complicated confection isn't easy, even for someone as super-organized as Ella. And her stepfamily just doesn't seem to understand how important this is to her. Ella could really use a fairy godmother right now. . . .

#6 *One Pet Too Many*

Paula's always loved animals, any animal. Who else would have a pet raccoon, not to mention three cats, three dogs, four finches, and fish? When Paula finds a lost armadillo, though, her parents say, "no more pets!"—and that's that. But how much trouble could an armadillo be? Plenty, as Paula discovers—especially when she's trying to keep it a secret from her parents.

#7 *Adventure in Walt Disney World:*
A Disney Girls Super Special

The Disney Girls are so excited. The three pairs of *best* best friends are going to spend a week together at Walt Disney World. Find out how the Disney Girls' magical wishes come true as they have the adventure of their lives.

#8 *Beauty's Revenge*

Isabelle is thrilled when she finds out that her beastly neighbor, Kenny, will be going away on vacation for a week with his family. Then Kenny comes down with chicken pox—and he has to stay at Isabelle's house for the week! She might be tempted to feel bad for Kenny—if he wasn't being his usual beastly self. With the help of the Disney Girls and a little magic, she decides to give Kenny a taste of *her* own medicine.

#9 *Good-bye, Jasmine?*

Jasmine has always been a little bit different from the other Disney Girls. She lives in the wealthy Wildwood Estates instead of in Willow Hill like her friends. But at least the girls get to see each other every day at Orlando Elementary. Then one day, Jasmine's mother decides that it's time for her daughter to attend her alma mater, St John's boarding school. The Disney Girls are in shock. Will they have to say good-bye to one of their best friends?